Mia
the Bridesmaid
Fairy

For Eloise Bishop,
a true friend of the fairies!

Special thanks to Rachel Elliot

ISBN 978-0-545-20251-0

12 11 10 9   13 14 15/0

Printed in the U.S.A.   40

First Scholastic Printing, March 2010

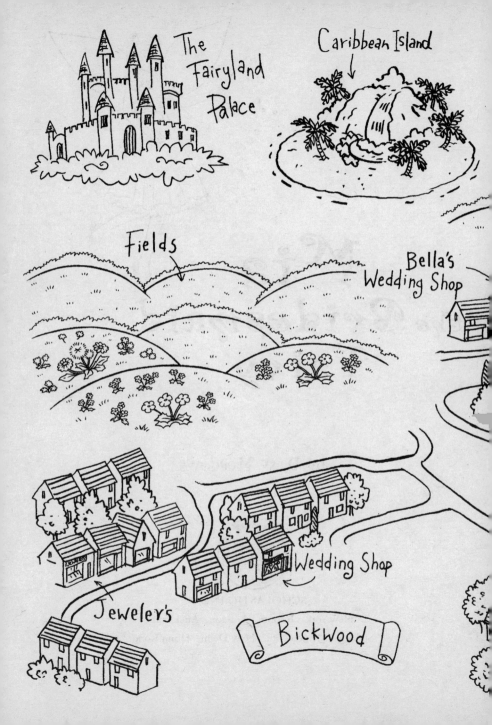

The Fairyland Palace

Caribbean Island

Fields

Bella's Wedding Shop

Jeweler's

Wedding Shop

Bickwood

Mia
the Bridesmaid
Fairy

by Daisy Meadows

SCHOLASTIC INC.

New York   Toronto   London   Auckland
Sydney   Mexico City   New Delhi   Hong Kong

Rain clouds brew and cold winds blow,
Seek out weddings high and low.
Blemish all the snow-white dresses,
Drizzle on their shining tresses.

Goblins, heed my cold command,
And travel to the human land.
These fairy charms I bid you hide,
To spoil the dreams of every bride!

**Find the hidden letters in the hearts
throughout this book. Unscramble all 7 letters
to spell a special wedding word!**

The Shiny Penny

Contents

"Look!" Rachel gasped in excitement.

They could see a large pool at the base of a frothing waterfall. And swinging across the pool on ropes, yelling, squealing, and screeching, was a gaggle of goblins!

Wedding Plans

"Isn't it exciting that we're going to be Esther's bridesmaids?" Rachel Walker said happily.

"Yes—I can hardly wait for next Saturday!" replied Kirsty Tate, smiling at her best friend. "And it'll be twice as much fun with you here!"

The girls were in Kenbury, the pretty

little village where Kirsty's cousin Esther had grown up. The sun was shining brightly and there wasn't a cloud in the sky. It was perfect wedding weather!

Esther, Mrs. Tate, and Aunt Isabel, Esther's mom, were in the nearby wedding dress store, but the girls had popped outside to look at the pretty church where Esther was going to get married.

"Oh, Kirsty, look!" cried Rachel. "There must be a wedding today!"

People were arriving in their best

clothes, carrying cameras and little boxes of confetti.

"And there's the pastor!" Kirsty added in excitement.

A lady in a long robe was standing near the church gate.

"Hello, girls," she said, smiling. "Are you here for the wedding?"

"Not today," said Kirsty, smiling back at her. "My cousin Esther is getting married here next Saturday, and we're her bridesmaids."

"We just got to see her wedding dress," added Rachel.

She pointed at a little store across the street. Above the window hung an old-fashioned sign:

Bella's WEDDING MAGIC

Rachel and Kirsty caught each other's eyes and grinned. They knew all about magic, because they shared an amazing secret. They were good friends with the fairies! They often helped them defeat mean Jack Frost and his naughty goblins.

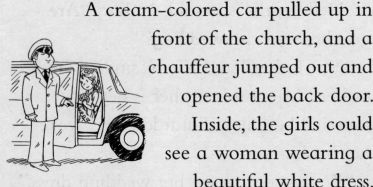

A cream-colored car pulled up in front of the church, and a chauffeur jumped out and opened the back door. Inside, the girls could see a woman wearing a beautiful white dress.

"It's the bride!" Rachel exclaimed.

"See you next week, girls." The pastor smiled. "I've got a wedding to perform!"

Rachel and Kirsty said good-bye and walked back to the wedding store.

"I love the dress in the window!" said Kirsty.

"Me, too," Rachel agreed.

Under an archway of roses, an exquisite wedding dress was surrounded by bouquets of real flowers.

"Bella's such an amazing dressmaker!" Kirsty said with a happy sigh.

Just then, Aunt Isabel popped her head out of the store's front door.

"Girls, come back inside," she said with a beaming smile. "Bella is ready for you to try on your dresses."

Rachel and Kirsty hurried to the room at the back of the store. Bella held up two amazing dresses, and the girls' eyes widened.

"Oh, they're beautiful!" Rachel whispered.

The two best friends quickly got changed, giggling with excitement. Then they stood in front of the long mirror.

"Oh, girls, you look fabulous!" cried Aunt Isabel.

"Just like princesses!" Esther added.

The dresses were pale blue, and they shimmered and sparkled with hundreds of tiny silver beads. Soft frills made the gowns swirl around the girls'  legs, and the sleeves were made from fine blue silk. They fluttered when the girls moved their arms.

"They're just like fairy wings!" Kirsty whispered to Rachel.

Bella checked to make sure the dresses fit properly, and made some small alterations.

"Thank you, girls," she said eventually. "You can get changed now."

"Our dresses are just gorgeous," sighed Rachel, smiling at Bella. "We love the one in the window, too. Is it waiting to be picked up?"

"No," said Bella. "It's a copy of one of my favorites, which I made a long time ago. I just couldn't bear to part with it, so I made another!"

"Wow, you must have made hundreds of dresses," said Aunt Isabel. "And I bet you know everything there is to know about weddings!"

"I've learned an awful lot," agreed Bella. "I love all the old traditions, and bridesmaids are one of the oldest traditions of all! It's their job to help things go smoothly for the bride."

Rachel and Kirsty exchanged happy looks.

"What other wedding traditions are there?" Rachel asked.

"Do you know what a bride is supposed to carry up the aisle to bring her luck?" asked Bella. "'Something old, something new, something borrowed, something blue, and a penny in her shoe.'"

"There's nothing wrong with a little

extra luck," said Esther, who had been trying on tiaras in front of the mirror. "Girls, will you be in charge of finding me these four 'somethings,' and a penny?"

"We'd love to!" Rachel said eagerly.

"Oh look, Rachel!" Kirsty exclaimed. "Let's start over there!"

At the front of the store, along the window, was a low table filled with wedding accessories.

The girls dashed over to it, while Mrs. Tate, Esther, and Aunt Isabel stayed at the back of the store.

"Look at these little bride and groom figures," said Kirsty. "They must go on the top of wedding cakes!"

"And here's a little bridesmaid figure!" cried Rachel in delight. "Oh, Kirsty, I can't wait to be a bridesmaid!"

"Me neither," Kirsty agreed.

"How about if Esther borrows the pretty dragonfly pin your mom's wearing for her something old?" Rachel suggested.

"That's perfect!" agreed Kirsty. "It's been in the family for years, so it's definitely old enough! Now we just have to think of something new, something borrowed, and something blue."

"And the penny for her shoe," Rachel reminded her. "Oh, Kirsty, look!"

She gave her best friend a nudge that made her squeak in surprise. The bridesmaid figure on the table had started to glow!

A Visitor From Fairyland

The sound of chimes echoed through
the air. Glittering fairy dust floated
down, and shining silver confetti
appeared where it landed. In place of
the bridesmaid figure stood a tiny fairy,
smiling up at the girls. Her dark pink
dress had a full skirt with a pale pink

bow, and a red rose glowed in her golden hair.

"Hello, girls," she said in a tiny voice. "I'm Mia the Bridesmaid Fairy!"

"Hi, Mia!" the girls replied excitedly. They moved closer to Mia so she couldn't be seen by the others.

"Is something wrong in Fairyland?" Rachel asked anxiously. The fairies often needed the girls' help when Jack Frost was causing trouble.

Mia gave them a warm smile. "Everything's fine. King Oberon and Queen Titania just asked me to sprinkle some extra good-luck fairy dust on your dresses so all the preparations for the wedding go well," she explained. "It's my job to make sure bridesmaids are happy, and that they make the wedding special!"

Before Kirsty and Rachel could reply, the church bells began to chime. Through the window the girls could see the wedding party outside, posing for a photograph.

Suddenly, a dark cloud covered the sun, and a gust of wind blew the bride's bouquet out of her hands! It tumbled toward a muddy puddle, and the bridesmaids ran after it.

"The bouquet will be ruined!" Kirsty gasped.

"And the bridesmaids will get mud on their pretty dresses!" Rachel exclaimed.

Just then, Mia sent a jet of sparkling magic from her wand. A magical breeze pushed the bouquet away from the puddle, and caused it to land safely on the grass. Rachel and Kirsty smiled in relief, but Mia shook her head and looked worried.

"That's funny," she said, frowning. "A

tiny bit of magic like
that shouldn't tire
me out, but I feel
weaker. I wonder if
something is wrong
with the three wedding
charms—those are what
give me my magic powers."

"You do look a little pale," Kirsty
noticed.

"Girls, will you come to Fairyland with
me?" asked Mia. "I need to find out what
the problem is before I do any more
magic."

"Of course we will!" said Rachel at
once.

Kirsty hurried to the back of the store.

"Mom, is it all right if we go now?" she
asked.

"OK," said Mrs. Tate. "We'll see you back at Aunt Isabel's house in half an hour."

Quickly, Kirsty and Rachel ran out of the store and down a cobblestone alley, with Mia hiding in Rachel's pocket. When they were out of sight, Mia waved her wand.

Immediately, a glittering stream of fairy dust burst from the wand's tip. It swirled around the girls, and they felt themselves shrinking to fairy-size!

Beautiful wings appeared on their backs.

"We're fairies again!" Rachel cried
in delight, fluttering in the air.

Mia waved her wand once more, and
glittering sparks spun around them like
a whirlwind. Soon, they had been
whisked away in a flurry of fairy dust.

When the magical sparkles faded, the girls were flying over Fairyland. Below, they could see red-and-white toadstool houses and the Fairyland Palace.

"Let's go straight to the Wedding Workshop, to see if we can find any clues about why I feel weak," Mia said. "It's inside the palace, so we can visit the king and queen after that."

"What happens in the Wedding Workshop?" asked Rachel.

"My fairy helpers make magical flower garlands and enchanted confetti, plus all sorts of other things that help weddings go smoothly," Mia explained. "It's also where we keep the three wedding charms. As long as they're in the workshop, my magic remains powerful." She led the girls into the

palace and fluttered down in front of
two white doors. "This is the best place
to find out what's wrong with my magic,
because—oh no!"

Mia pushed the doors open. The girls
saw long tables scattered with ribbons,
strings of pearls, and silks and satins in
all colors of the rainbow. But there wasn't
a fairy to be seen. The workshop was
deserted!

Goblin Mischief

"I don't understand!" cried Mia, looking around in shock. "The workshop never closes!"

"Let's go see the king and queen," Kirsty suggested. "I'm sure that they'll know what's going on."

Rachel, Kirsty, and Mia flitted quickly to the palace throne room. Inside, several anxious-looking fairies surrounded the king and queen. Rachel and Kirsty curtsied.

"Hello, Your Majesties," Rachel said politely.

"We're very glad to see you, girls," said Queen Titania in her silvery voice. "These are the other fairies who work with Mia in the workshop."

Each fairy curtsied to the girls, but they all looked miserable!

"Why is the workshop closed, Your Majesties?" asked Mia.

"Everything the fairies try to make falls apart," said King Oberon sadly.

"Yesterday was a fairy wedding party," Queen Titania explained to Rachel and Kirsty. "We have one every year to thank the fairies in the Wedding Workshop for all their hard work. I'll show you what happened."

She led them to the Seeing Pool in the palace gardens and waved her wand over the glassy surface. The water swirled like a whirlpool. When it settled, a picture appeared.

Lots of fairies, goblins, elves, and

pixies were dancing inside the palace ballroom. A string quartet of frog musicians played wonderful music.

"Look, there's Jack Frost!" cried Rachel.

Tall, icy Jack Frost was standing alone in the corner of the ballroom. His arms  were folded, and he had a sulky expression on his face. He beckoned to some of his goblins and led them into the dining hall. Inside, tall cakes towered over platters of cream puffs, cupcakes, ice cream cones, and colorful Jell-O. There were melt-in-your-mouth pastries, chocolate fountains, and even a swan ice sculpture with candy in the hollow of its back.

"This will teach them not to ask me to dance!" snarled Jack Frost. "Eat up!"

With a cheer of greedy delight, the goblins hurled themselves at the feast. The tall cakes splattered to the floor, while Jell-O and ice cream whizzed through the air. Some of the goblins even jumped into a chocolate fountain!

"Jack Frost!" cried a voice.

The king and queen stood in the doorway, looking angry.

"You were a welcome guest in our palace, but now you have spoiled the feast for everyone!" said the queen.

"When I attend a party, I expect all the attention!" bellowed Jack Frost.

In the picture, Mia appeared behind the king and queen.

"This is a wedding party!" she cried.

"The fairies from the Wedding Workshop are the guests of honor, not you!"

"Be quiet, you silly fairy!" Jack Frost snapped.

"You and your goblins need to learn that greediness and bad manners don't pay," said King Oberon sternly. "Go home. You are not welcome at the rest of the celebration."

Enraged, Jack Frost pointed a thin, icy finger at Mia.

"*You'll* regret this!" he hissed.

With that, the image faded from the Seeing Pool.

"While Mia was on her way to visit Rachel and Kirsty earlier today, Jack Frost ambushed the Wedding Workshop. He stole the wedding charms and sent his goblins to hide them in the human world," said Queen Titania gravely.

Mia's eyes filled with tiny, sparkling tears.

"*All* of them?" she asked in a trembling voice.

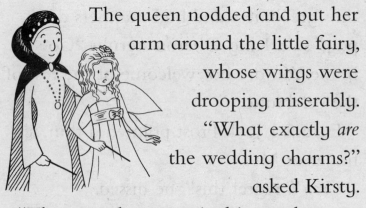

The queen nodded and put her arm around the little fairy, whose wings were drooping miserably.

"What exactly *are* the wedding charms?" asked Kirsty.

"They are three magical items that help recharge Mia's magic powers," the queen explained. "They also make weddings go smoothly. The shiny penny ensures that the married couple will prosper all their lives."

"The golden bells are a good luck

charm," added the king. "And the silver veil brings happiness."

"But without the charms, Mia's powers will weaken and disappear," the queen finished.

"Oh no!" Rachel gasped, clasping Mia's hand.

"This could ruin every wedding in the human world!" Mia cried.

The Wishing Well

"Mia, do you think you can find the charms before it's too late?" asked the queen.

"I'll do everything I can," said Mia, sounding determined.

"We'll help!" the girls chimed in eagerly.

The queen smiled. "I was hoping you would say that!"

"How will we know where to start looking?" asked Rachel.

"I have a special connection to the charms," explained Mia. "The closer I am to them, the stronger my magic feels. That should help us to find them."

"Let's start looking right away," said Kirsty. "There's no time to lose!"

Queen Titania smiled at the girls gratefully and waved her wand. "Good luck!" she said.

"Thank you— good-bye!" called Rachel and Kirsty together.

Mia and the girls disappeared in a glittering whirl of fairy dust.

A moment later, they found themselves back in the alley in Kenbury.

"Will you tell us more about each charm so we can work out a plan?" Rachel asked Mia eagerly.

"Well," Mia began, "the shiny penny is the least powerful of the charms. Its magic is usually used to help couples prosper, but in the wrong hands it could be used to steal money."

"And greedy goblin hands are definitely the wrong hands!" said Kirsty with a sigh.

Suddenly, Mia gave a cry of excitement. She rose above them, flitting left and right.

"I can sense that the shiny penny has been here!" she gasped. "If we hurry, we can follow the goblins!"

Quickly, Mia flew off and the girls followed her. Soon they were flitting over pretty purple flowers in a large field. Mia pointed at a small village up ahead.

"The shiny penny is there somewhere," she declared. "I'm sure of it."

As they fluttered toward the village, Rachel gave a surprised cry.

"I came here on vacation once!" she said excitedly. "This village is famous because it has the oldest wishing well in the country!"

Kirsty gasped, understanding her best friend at once. "In the human world, people throw *coins* into wishing wells," she explained to Mia.

"Maybe the goblins have seen humans making wishes, and now they're trying to use the shiny penny to wish for

36

more money!" Rachel added eagerly.

Sure enough, they soon spotted a group of goblins standing around the wishing well, arguing loudly. The girls landed close by and hid behind a tree trunk.

"You fool!" they heard one goblin snap. "Why did you throw it in there?"

"I wished for all the money in the world, but nothing happened!" wailed another, who had a large wart on his nose.

"The shiny penny would never respond to a greedy wish like that!" whispered Mia indignantly.

"So now we have NO money and NO shiny penny!" roared a third goblin, poking the warty one in the chest with his long finger. "Do you want to explain that to Jack Frost, pea-brain?"

"You have to get it back," the first goblin declared.

"Not me!" squealed the warty one. "I'm scared of the dark!"

"Tough luck," said another goblin. "You should have thought of that before!"

He grabbed the warty goblin's ankles and dangled him upside down over the well.

"Eeek! Let me go!"
shrieked the goblin.

But another goblin
seized the second one's
ankles and dangled him
into the well, too. The
warty one dropped down
even lower.

"NO!" he wailed, his
voice echoing.

One by one, each
goblin grabbed the ankles
of the goblin in front, making a bony,
green chain out of their own bodies.

"You're squeezing my ankles too hard!"
yelled one.

"Being upside down makes me dizzy!"
another complained. "I feel sick!"

39

"Stop complaining and get on with it!" bellowed the goblin at the top of the well, who had to hold on to them all.

With groans and moans, they slowly lowered the warty goblin down near the very bottom of the well.

"We have to find the shiny penny before they do," Kirsty whispered urgently. "But how?"

"I've got an idea!" Rachel said suddenly, her eyes gleaming. "Mia, can you use your magic to make some fake shiny pennies?"

"Yes," said Mia. "My magic powers are stronger because the real penny is so close. But how will that help?"

"If we can confuse the goblins with the fake coins, we'll have a better chance of getting our hands on the real shiny penny!" Rachel explained.

"That's a great plan!" cried Mia in excitement. "And I can use my fairy magic to make the coins disappear as soon as the goblins touch them. Come on!"

Mia and the girls flitted toward the dark well. Rachel's heart began to thump. Could they trick the goblins—without getting caught?

"Fairies!" shrieked one goblin, as Mia and the girls entered the well. "Don't let them find the coin!"

The goblin chain still hadn't reached the water at the bottom of the well. But the second goblin let go of the warty one's ankles, and he fell the rest of the way down, howling loudly. He landed in the water with a loud splash.

"Quick, find it!" shouted the other goblins, who were still dangling down the side of the well.

Mia and the girls hovered just above the water. Then Mia waved her wand and created a fake penny.

"Got it!" she called loudly, holding it up to show the goblins.

Coin Confusion

Mia fluttered away from the goblin, clutching the fake coin. The other goblins yelled instructions as loud as they could.

"After her!"

"Stop her!"

"Faster!"

Confused by all the shouting, the goblin chased Mia around and around

the inside of the well, while Kirsty and
Rachel dived underwater. None of the
goblins were watching them. Their plan
was working!

The bottom of the well was covered
in coins, but one had a
beautiful bronze glow.
The girls were sure
that it was the real
shiny penny, and they
carefully picked it up.

Meanwhile, the goblin
finally caught up with Mia and snatched
the fake penny out of her hand. But as
soon as his clammy fingers touched the
coin, it disappeared! The other goblins gave
howls of rage.

Just then, Rachel and Kirsty rose out of
the water and nodded at Mia. She flicked

her wand and a fake coin appeared in Rachel's hands, while Kirsty hid the real shiny penny behind her back.

"*She's* got it!" yelled one of the goblins, pointing at Rachel.

All the goblins' eyes turned toward Rachel. They didn't pay any attention to Kirsty as she flew swiftly out of the well, carrying the real shiny penny. Rachel pretended that the fake coin was too heavy for her.

"Help!" she called to Mia. "I'm not strong enough!"

"I'm coming!" Mia cried.

"Get her!" the goblins yelled.

The warty goblin flung himself toward Rachel, but she flew out of his reach just in time! She flapped upward, pretending to pant with the effort.

"NO!" screamed the other goblins. "She's getting away!"

"Come down and help me, then!" snapped the warty goblin, jumping up and down and trying to catch Rachel.

The goblin at the top of the well swung the goblin chain, and all five dangling goblins let go at once. They launched themselves at Rachel in a jumble of arms and legs. Then the goblin at the top of the well jumped down too, aiming for Rachel and her coin!

Rachel flung herself against the side of the well and dropped the fake coin. All the goblins splash-landed in a green, tangled heap at the bottom of the well.

"Find that coin!" spluttered the warty goblin from the bottom of the pile.

Giggling, Mia and Rachel fluttered up and out of the well.

"Those pesky fairies are getting away!" shrieked another goblin.

"Never mind them!" yelled a third, scrambling around in the water. "Find the shiny penny!"

Kirsty was waiting at the top of the well, holding the real penny and grinning.

"It worked like a charm!" Rachel laughed.

"Thank you so much for helping me," said Mia. "I feel stronger already!"

With a touch of her wand, she returned the coin to its Fairyland size. Then she put it into a little silk pouch that she tucked

in a pocket of her dress. The shouts of the goblins below echoed around the well.

"Let's go!" Mia advised. "It won't be long before they realize they've been tricked!"

Sure enough, as the girls flew away, they heard a chorus of enraged shrieks.

"I think they just found the last fake coin—and it vanished!" Kirsty giggled.

Back in Kenbury, near Aunt Isabel's house, Mia returned the girls to their normal size.

"I'm going to take the shiny penny back to its home in the Wedding Workshop!" she said happily. "Thank you so much, girls. I'm sure I'll see you again very soon. We still have a difficult task ahead — we need to find the other two charms!"

Rachel and Kirsty nodded and waved good-bye.

"I'm so glad that we found the shiny penny!" Rachel grinned.

"Me, too," Kirsty replied. "I just hope that we can find the other charms before Saturday!"

"Don't worry, we won't let Jack Frost spoil Esther's wedding," said Rachel, nodding firmly. "We've got Mia to help us, and we've got each other. We can help save the day!"

51

The Golden Bells

Contents

A Charming Challenge

"I can't believe how many things there are to think about for just one wedding," Kirsty said, peering into a display case in the jewelry store. "I'm not surprised that Mia needs help in the Wedding Workshop!"

That morning, Esther and her mom had taken the girls to Bickwood, the nearby town. Esther needed some jewelry to wear when she left for her honeymoon.

"These necklaces are so pretty," said Rachel.

"They look as delicate as if they had been made by fairies!" Kirsty replied.

"Maybe Esther could use the necklace she buys today as the something new?" Rachel suggested.

"But it's for her honeymoon, not for the wedding." Kirsty sighed. Then her eyes brightened. "But Esther's wedding dress has been made especially for her! That could be the something new!"

"Perfect!" Rachel exclaimed. "Now we just have to find something borrowed and something blue!"

They stopped next to a table where some pretty jewelry boxes and pouches were displayed.

"I bet India the Moonstone Fairy would love this store," Kirsty said quietly to Rachel, remembering the adventures they had shared with the Jewel Fairies. "And—oh!"

A purple, velvet jewelry pouch had fallen off the table and landed on the floor in front of them. Rachel picked it up. "Kirsty, look!" she exclaimed. Two gold initials were sewn on the pouch—

R and K . . . for Rachel and Kirsty?

Kirsty's eyes shone. "Do you think it might be magic?"

Rachel nodded excitedly and opened the pouch. Mia flew out

in a flurry of fairy dust!

"Hello, girls!" she whispered, fluttering over to hide on Kirsty's shoulder.

The girls quickly moved to a quiet part of the store, where no one could overhear them.

"Mia!" whispered Kirsty in delight. "How are you?"

"Not great," Mia admitted. "Things are going wrong at weddings everywhere!"

"At least the poor bridesmaids have you to help them," said Rachel.

"Yes, and I'm feeling stronger now that the shiny penny is safe, even though my magic is still not as powerful as usual," said Mia. "But girls, I think the goblins have taken the golden bells to a Caribbean island!"

"How can you be sure?" asked Rachel.

"The island is popular for beach weddings," Mia explained. "That's where some of the unluckiest things have been happening so far, and the golden bells control luck. Will you come and help me look for them?"

"Of course!" replied Rachel eagerly.

Kirsty hurried over to her cousin and aunt.

"Aunt Isabel, can we go off by ourselves for a while?" she asked. "We want to look for something that will make Esther's wedding extra special."

"Yes, all right, dear," Aunt Isabel said, smiling. "But don't be long."

Kirsty and Rachel hurried outside and dashed up an alleyway. As they did, Mia waved her wand and sprinkled fairy dust over them. Immediately, the girls shrank to fairy-size and fluttered their wings in delight. However many wonderful adventures they shared with their fairy friends, it was always thrilling to be able to fly!

"We must get to the island as quickly as we can," said Mia.

She flicked her wand again, and a puffy white cloud drifted toward them. By the time it reached them, it had transformed into a gleaming white carriage, pulled by four white cloud horses!

Luck of the Leprechaun

Mia and the girls climbed into the carriage, and the horses whisked them through the blue sky. Rachel and Kirsty snuggled back in their seats. They could feel the cloud shape itself around them as Mia told them the story of the golden bells.

"Many years ago, King Oberon rescued a leprechaun from some goblins who were playing tricks on him," Mia said.

"He was lost and tired, so the king gave him good food and a warm bed. Before the leprechaun left, he gave the king two of the lucky gold bells from his hat to thank him."

"What a nice present!" said Kirsty, her eyes shining.

"The king wanted everyone to share in the leprechaun's gift," Mia went on. "So he gave the bells to me, to bring luck to all weddings."

"Kirsty, we have to find the golden bells!" said Rachel. "We can't let Jack Frost and his goblins use all that luck for themselves!"

They felt the carriage sinking lower in the sky. After a gentle bump, the door opened and they tumbled out onto the white sand of a Caribbean beach. With a wave of Mia's wand, the cloud horses whinnied and pulled the carriage off into the air again. As they went, they seemed to lose their shape. Soon, they were just ordinary clouds again.

Mia was looking pale. "I'm feeling a little weak," she said. "That used up more magic than I thought it would."

"Don't worry," said Kirsty, squeezing her hand. "We'll find the golden bells soon and recharge your magic."

The girls brushed the fine sand off their clothes and gazed around in delight. Tall palm trees waved in a warm breeze, and sunlight glittered on the foaming waves.

"This is the most amazing beach I've ever seen!" Kirsty smiled in awe.

"Maybe the luck of the golden bells will help us find them right away," said Rachel. "Then we'll have time to explore!"

But Mia's wings drooped sadly. "The luck only works for whoever last touched the golden bells," she said. "And of course, that was the goblins."

Kirsty and Rachel exchanged determined looks.

"Don't worry, Mia," said Rachel, putting her arm around the little fairy's shoulders. "We'll get the golden bells back from those pesky goblins!"

"Luck might be on our side after all!" said Kirsty, pointing farther down the beach.

A group of goblins was playing beach volleyball, running around in brightly patterned shorts. One was wearing flippers on his feet, and another had swimming goggles around his head. Suntan lotion was smeared all over their noses and cheeks.

Suddenly, the goblin
in flippers tripped
over his feet and
missed the ball.

"Ten points
to us!" shouted a
goblin in a flowery
swimming cap.

"No, it isn't!" snapped the goblin
wearing flippers.

Looking furious,
the first goblin
pushed him over.
"I'll get you for
that!" the one in
flippers shrieked
with rage.
He flung
himself at the

other goblin and they rolled around on
the sand, yelling and fighting. The other
goblins piled on top of them.

Rachel shook her head in amazement.
"They must really enjoy arguing,
because they even do it on vacation!" she
exclaimed.

Then she gasped and pointed down the
beach. On a long ribbon, dangling from
a nearby
palm tree,
were the
golden
bells!

Hide-and-Seek

The girls and Mia immediately fluttered toward the palm tree, staying low to the ground and out of sight. Lizards and hermit crabs scurried out of their way.

"Over here!" whispered Rachel, ducking behind a large fallen coconut under the tree.

Kirsty and Mia joined her and glanced over at the goblins. The argument was over and they had started to play volleyball again. In the meantime, the girls were almost directly underneath the golden bells!

"I could just fly up and get them!" said Mia eagerly.

"Wait—what if the goblins see you?" Kirsty wondered aloud.

But Mia rose off the ground, and Kirsty and Rachel held their breath. Mia's fingers had almost reached the golden bells when . . .

THUMP!

A volleyball banged against

the tree, flinging the golden bells into the air. With a chiming sound, they landed in the arms of a goblin wearing shorts that were patterned with blue daisies. Rachel and Kirsty flew up to join Mia, and the goblin spotted them.

"Fairies!" he shouted.

"They can't do anything!" sneered another, who was wearing bright orange water wings. "Luck is on our side!"

Oh no, they know about the luck! Rachel thought, groaning.

"Let's go and play somewhere else," said the blue-daisy goblin.

"Wait!" cried Rachel desperately. "Can't you see that you're ruining weddings everywhere?"

"Can't *you* see that *we* don't care?" jeered the goblin.

"I think it's better if they don't see anything at all!" said another in a mocking, singsong voice. He picked up a handful of sand and threw it at the girls and Mia!

"Close your eyes!" Mia cried.

Rachel and Kirsty squeezed their eyes shut as the sand rained down on them. They could hear snickering and footsteps. But when they opened their eyes again, the goblins were nowhere to be seen.

"They must have run away!" Kirsty said, annoyed.

"It's the luck of the golden bells working against us," said Mia sadly. "But we have to find them . . . and fast!"

Mia and the girls fluttered over trees, peered into caves, and flew around rocks and bushes, keeping their eyes peeled for a glint of goblin green or a flash of gold. But the longer they looked, the paler Mia became.

"I feel really tired," she said with a sigh. "It took a lot of magical energy to bring us here, and we've been searching for a long

time. I'll have to go back to Fairyland and use the shiny penny to recharge my magic."

"Wait!" said Rachel, holding up her hand. "Can you hear something?"

They all paused and listened. Kirsty nodded eagerly.

"It sounds like . . . goblins!" she said.

Kirsty, Rachel, and Mia flew around a cluster of tall palm trees.

Treetop Trouble

"Oh, those terrible goblins!" Mia exclaimed. "They're making such a scene."

"Whoopee!" yelled two goblins, cannonballing into the pool.

Fish swam out of the way and flamingos scattered in confusion as the goblins' screeches echoed around the clearing.

"Geronimo!" hollered another goblin. He somersaulted under the waterfall, splashing water onto the banks. A flock of parrots rose into the air, squawking angrily.

There seemed to be goblins everywhere! But where were the golden bells?

"Let's fly around the pool and see if Mia can sense which direction the bells were taken," said Kirsty.

They started to flutter around the pool, holding Mia's hands to help her along. Suddenly, she gave a gasp. "I felt a prickle of magic all down my back!" she exclaimed. "The golden bells must be in that direction!" said Rachel, pointing. The three friends fluttered away from the pool, and soon Mia let go of the girls' hands. "I'm feeling stronger already," she said.

"We're getting closer!"

After flying for a few more minutes, they reached a clearing and Kirsty gave a cry. There was a glint of gold amidst the green! The golden bells were hanging from their ribbon on a high branch, but . . .

"Oh no!" Rachel whispered.

Two goblin guards were there, too, clutching the branch tightly. They were so pale green that they were almost white!

"You have more room than me!" whimpered the first goblin, who

had swimming goggles around his head.

"I don't have any room at all!" The other goblin trembled, still wearing his flowery swimming cap.

"It was your silly idea to draw straws to decide who would guard the golden bells," the goggled goblin said.

"But why did you have to hide them in the tallest tree?" The other one gulped, looking down and then covering his eyes.

"Hey, stop pushing me!" the first goblin complained.

"You're the one pushing me!" whined

the second goblin, giving him a shove.

Just then, they both lost their grip on the branch and tumbled backward out of the tree!

The goblin with the flowery cap hooked his toe over a branch below. He grabbed the other goblin by his swimming trunks. Now they both dangled upside down.

Rachel gasped. "That was lucky!"

Mia nodded. "It was the luck of the golden bells."

"You made my goggles fall off!" the

first goblin wailed, clambering back up
to the branch.

"You pushed us off the branch in the
first place!" grumbled the goblin in
the swimming cap.

"Did not!"

"Did so!"

They started to climb back up the tree,
bickering as they went.

"Now's our chance!" Kirsty said.

"I'll fly to the end of the branch and unhook the golden bells," said Mia.

But Rachel shook her head. "We can't," she said firmly. "If we fly away with the golden bells, the goblins' luck will change. They'll probably fall out of the tree and hurt themselves!"

"You're right," said Mia, her shoulders sagging.

"Mia, can you use your magic to get the goblins to the ground safely?" asked Kirsty.

"Yes," said Mia. "But only if I've touched the golden bells. I need their luck on my side."

"Then that's what you'll have to do," Kirsty declared. "Touch the golden bells, and use magic to get the goblins safely to the ground before they can grab us!"

"You'll have to be quick," added Rachel in alarm. "They've almost reached the branch again!"

Something Blue

As the goblins lunged for the branch, Mia and the girls flew up to the bells and tried to tug the ribbon loose. Shrieking with rage, the goblins swatted the girls away.

"Help!" cried Kirsty. "My wings are tangled and I'm falling!"

The girls and goblins all lost their

balance and went tumbling toward the ground, a jumble of arms, legs, and wings!

"Fairies, use your magic!" the goblins yelped.

"My wand arm is trapped!" Mia cried.

THUMP! They all landed in a heap on a soft pile of moss and leaves. There was a chiming sound as the golden bells landed nearby.

"Hang on . . ." said Rachel, untangling her wings from the goblins' legs.

"Wait a minute . . ." said one of the goblins.

"Who was the last one to touch the golden bells?" they cried together.

They had no idea whose side the luck was on!

The goblins and the girls all made a dash for the golden bells at exactly the same moment. But one of the goblins tripped on a root, and

the other stubbed his toe on a rock. Mia reached the golden bells first, and the girls realized that it must have been Mia who had touched them last. Luck was on her side!

The goblins gave angry cries as they hopped around the clearing, clutching their sore toes.

"I'm not explaining this to Jack Frost!" wailed the first one.

"Me, neither!" the other declared.

With that, they disappeared into the forest. As their voices faded away, Rachel and Kirsty sighed with relief.

Just then, something twirled down from the sky and landed next to Kirsty. She picked it up.

"Look!" she said. "It's a feather!"

The feather was a bright blue color that shimmered and gleamed in the sunlight.

"Oh, Rachel!" Kirsty exclaimed suddenly. "This can be our something blue for Esther!"

99

"You're right!" Rachel agreed, smiling widely.

"Thank you both so much for helping me find the golden bells!" Mia said gratefully.

With a twirl of her wand, she turned the golden bells back to their Fairyland size and put them in a silk pouch, which she tucked into her dress.

Then she grinned and gave another wave of her wand. Rachel and Kirsty closed their eyes as a whirl of sparkling confetti surrounded them. When they opened their eyes again, they were standing on a quiet street next to the jewelry store in Bickwood.

"Thank you again, girls," said Mia. "I'm going to hurry back to Fairyland and return the golden bells. But I'll see you very soon—after all, we still need to find the silver veil!"

She disappeared in a flurry of sparkles, and the girls walked back into the store.

"Hi, girls!" Esther called. "Come and tell me which earrings to choose. I can't decide!"

Rachel and Kirsty hurried over and looked at all the jewelry in the case. There were diamond studs, dangling

pendants, and pretty flower shapes. But Rachel and Kirsty knew exactly which ones to pick. They both pointed at a pair of earrings in the shape of tiny, golden bells!

The Silver Veil

Contents

Shooting Star

"Just one more night to go!" said Kirsty as she brushed her hair. "Isn't it exciting?"

Rachel nodded eagerly, and then sighed. "But I won't be able to really enjoy it if we haven't found the silver veil," she said, climbing into bed. "I'll be too worried about the trouble Jack Frost and his goblins will cause."

"That's true," agreed Kirsty, looking thoughtful.

The door opened, and Mrs. Tate popped her head in the room.

"Are you ready for bed, girls?" she asked.

"Yes, Mom," said Kirsty. "Is everything OK downstairs?"

"I think so!" Mrs. Tate laughed. "I've been practicing hairstyles on your Aunt Isabel while she double-checked the seating plans. Esther is finishing up some details with her friends."

"It sounds like the whole village of Kenbury is here

tonight!" said Rachel with a grin.

The house had been packed with
friends, family, and neighbors all day,
and the sound of laughter still floated up
the stairs.

"We're all helping to make sure
everything is ready to go," said Mrs. Tate
with a smile.

"Like what, Mom?" Kirsty asked.

"Oh, all the hundreds of tiny
details that go into making
the perfect wedding," said
Mrs. Tate with a wink.
"Goodnight, girls. I'll
see you bright and
early in the morning!"

She turned off the
main light and closed the
door behind her.

"I keep thinking about all the things that could go *wrong* tomorrow," Kirsty said after a moment.

"Me, too," Rachel added nervously, sitting up in bed. "Unless we find the silver veil, anything could happen at the wedding. It's bound to be something to do with us bridesmaids."

"And we still haven't thought of the something borrowed for Esther," Kirsty said, walking over to the window and opening it. "But let's try not to worry too much. I'm sure we can help Esther have the perfect day!"

She leaned out and breathed in the
fresh country air. In the distance,
she could see the lights of Bickwood
twinkling. Rachel joined her. Together,
they looked up at the moonlit,
star-filled sky.

"You can always see ten times as many
stars in the country," said Kirsty.

"I know," Rachel agreed. "Oh,
Kirsty — look!"

She pointed up to where a shooting
star was burning across the sky.

"Quick, make a wish!" Kirsty exclaimed.

They both closed their eyes and made their wishes. But when they opened their eyes again, Kirsty frowned.

"That's funny," she said. "The shooting star isn't fading. It seems to be getting bigger."

Sure enough, the burning star was getting brighter . . . and brighter . . . and brighter!

"It's coming straight at us!" Rachel
cried.

As the girls jumped aside, the star shot
between them onto the carpet, fizzing
and crackling. When it faded, Mia was
standing in front of them, smiling
as brightly as the star itself!

A Fake Feast

"Hello again, girls!" called Mia.

"Hi, Mia!" Rachel and Kirsty cried in delight.

"Have you found the silver veil?" asked Kirsty hopefully.

"Not yet," Mia replied. "But this is the best time to search for it. In the dark, it glows just like the moon. Plus, there's a lunar eclipse tonight!"

Rachel frowned. "What's that?"

"The Earth is going to pass between the moon and the sun," said Mia, creating a magical picture with her wand to show what this looked like.  "It will block the light from the sun, and Earth's shadow will cover the moon. That means that we'll be able to spot the light from the silver veil even more easily."

"But we still don't know where the veil is," Kirsty said.

Suddenly, Rachel's eyes lit up.

"I've got an idea," she said. "We all know that the greedy goblins can't resist food. Mia, do you think you could use your magic to make a delicious feast?"

"Yes," said Mia. "But how will a feast help?"

"If the goblins are nearby, I'm sure that they'll try to steal the food," Rachel explained.

"You're right!" Kirsty cried.

"It's a little dangerous to lead the goblins to us on purpose," Mia warned them.

Rachel and Kirsty looked at each other. It was kind of scary to think about facing lots of goblins, but if they didn't find the silver veil tonight, Esther's wedding might be ruined!

"We have to risk it!" Rachel said determinedly.

So Mia swished her wand, and glittering fairy dust whirled around the girls.

They felt themselves shrinking to fairy-size, and they fluttered their wings with excitement. Then they flew through the window, down the lane, and out of the village to a dark, empty glade. The three of them landed next to a clump of daisies.

In no time, Mia flicked her wand and a marvelous feast appeared. Delicious food was laid out on a large blanket. There were piles of cucumber sandwiches, hot baked potatoes with melting butter and cheese, jugs of lemonade, chocolate cupcakes, and bowls filled with strawberries and cream.

"Now all we can do is wait," said Mia.

Almost as soon as they had hidden behind the daisies, the three friends heard jabbering voices. A group of goblins walked across the field. All of them were carrying backpacks, and the girls could see a large net poking out of one of them.

Rachel nudged Kirsty and pointed. One of the backpacks was glowing silvery-blue!

"The silver veil!" Kirsty exclaimed.

As soon as the goblins greedily reached for the food, it disappeared! Mia, Rachel, and Kirsty fluttered out from their hiding place and faced the goblins.

"Give back the veil!" Mia demanded. "It doesn't belong to you!"

"You tricky fairies!" the tallest goblin yelped, scowling.

"Please give back the veil," Kirsty said. "Mia will reward you with as many cakes as you can eat."

"Mmm, cakes," said a plump goblin. "I like the sound of that."

"It's a trick!" said the tall goblin. "The cakes will vanish, just like the feast!"

"But I'm really hungry!" wailed the first one. "Let's give them the silly veil!"

Mia and Kirsty were distracted by the squabbling goblins, but Rachel suddenly turned pale.

"Kirsty," she said, "how many goblins did you see come into the field?"

"Um . . . seven," Kirsty replied. "Why?"

"Because now there are only five of them," Rachel said, alarmed.

They whirled around—just as the two remaining goblins threw the net over them from behind!

Eclipse of the Moon

The other goblins stopped fighting and tied the net shut with a rope.

"Oh no!" whispered Mia. "I dropped my wand!"

"Tee-hee!" giggled the tall goblin. "We tricked the tricky fairies!"

They snickered and waved at Mia and the girls, who were squashed together in

the net. Then they
ran off toward
Bickwood.

"*Ouch!*"
exclaimed
Rachel. "I
think you've
got your elbow in my ear, Kirsty."

"Sorry," said Kirsty, moving it.

"Ooh, now it's in *my* ear!" said Mia.

"Sorry!" cried Kirsty again. "Oh, what
are we going to do?"

"Mia, can you use your magic to get
us out of here?" asked Rachel.

"Not without my wand." Mia sighed.

"We've got to get out of here fast,
or the goblins will escape!" Rachel
exclaimed.

"Girls," Mia said suddenly. "Listen!"

They went silent, and heard a loud snuffling noise. A brown field mouse was scurrying toward them.

"Excuse me," called Mia. "Can you please help us? We're stuck!"

The little mouse sat up on its back legs and sniffed the air. Its whiskers twitched. Then it hurried over and nibbled at the net. Soon it had made a hole large enough for the friends to clamber through.

As Mia picked up her wand, she kissed the tip of the field mouse's

nose. "Thank you so much!" she whispered.
Mia waved her wand, and a pile of nuts
and berries appeared in front of the
happy mouse.

Then the three friends fluttered their
crumpled wings and rose into the air.
As they flew toward Bickwood, the

night seemed to grow darker.

"The eclipse of the moon is almost complete!" Rachel cried.

As the Earth's shadow finally covered the moon, one street was still bathed in light.

"*That's* where the silver veil is!" cried Mia in triumph.

"And the goblins!" Rachel reminded her.

The light was coming from a wedding store. The girls quickly flew down, peered through the window — and gasped.

The shop was crawling with goblins, all wearing veils, wedding dresses, hats, and high heels! One of them was walking with his arms held out, balancing a pile of wobbling tiaras on his head.

Another was wearing a gold tuxedo. He was poking a goblin in a pink frilly bridesmaid dress.

"Get away!" yelled the goblin in the dress.

He tried to kick, but his foot got caught in the dress and he tripped over himself.

Rachel, Kirsty, and Mia slipped into the store through the mail slot and fluttered to hide behind a large hat. Somewhere among those puffy dresses, pink frills, and dressed-up goblins was the silver veil . . . but where?

A Visit From Jack Frost?

"I bet Jack Frost would be furious if he could see the goblins goofing off!" Mia said.

"You just gave me an idea!" Kirsty exclaimed. "Mia, could you make my voice sound like Jack Frost's?"

Mia nodded thoughtfully, then waved her wand toward Kirsty.

"Did it work?" Kirsty asked in a growly whisper.

"You sound exactly like him!" Rachel gasped.

"You'd better be quick," Mia said. "The magic won't last long."

Kirsty took a deep breath.

"What are you doing, you fools?" she bellowed.

The goblins froze in terror.

"You should be hiding the silver veil, not enjoying yourselves!" Kirsty roared.

The goblins looked around wildly.

"W–we w–were
j–just about to h–hide
it, s–sir!" stammered
the goblin in the
wedding dress.

"You're useless!"
Kirsty shouted. "Give
me the silver veil, or I'll
turn you all into goblin ice sculptures!"

Trembling, the goblin pulled a
shimmering square of material from the
bodice of the wedding dress. Mia darted
forward to grab it, but Rachel stopped
her.

"Not yet!" she whispered.

"Put it on the floor!" ordered Kirsty in
a booming voice. "Then turn around!"

The goblins obeyed, and the girls flew

out from their hiding place to grab the
veil.

"Now shut your eyes!" Kirsty shouted.

But her voice cracked—the spell was
wearing off! The goblins turned around,
saw the girls, and immediately rushed
forward. Hands pulled at the silver veil
from all sides.

"It's going to rip!" Mia exclaimed. "We
have to let go! We can't
let it be ruined!"

In despair, Mia
and the girls
let go. But the
goblins weren't
expecting
that! They
all tumbled
backward, and
the silver veil flew
into the air.

"Quick, Mia!" Kirsty called out.

As Mia darted up and caught it, the
veil shrank back down to fairy-size.

The girls looked down and giggled.
The goblins had fallen backward and

crashed into racks of wedding dresses. All that the girls could see were seven pairs of green legs waving in the air, surrounded by dresses, ribbons, and veils.

"Get me out of here!" yelled a muffled voice from under a heap of lace.

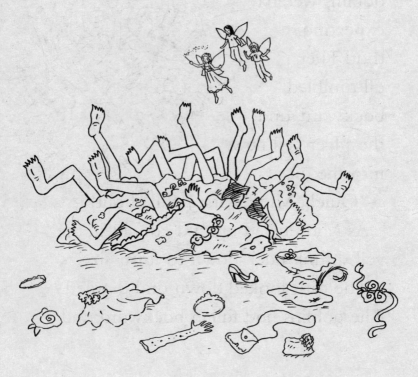

Mia and the girls flew quickly out of the mail slot and landed gently on the pavement outside the store.

"Thank you, girls!" Mia said. "I'll make sure that the store is all cleaned up before morning. But first, I have to return the silver veil to Fairyland!"

"I've never seen anything shine like that before," said Rachel.

She and Kirsty gently touched the veil. It was so fine that they could hardly feel it

under their fingers, and it lit up their
faces with its sparkling light. It made
them feel safe and warm just to look
at it.

"It belonged to
a very happy
bride," Mia told
them. "The
first Queen
of Fairyland.
It's made from
moonlight, and
happiness is woven inside its threads."

She folded the veil into the tiniest
square Rachel and Kirsty could imagine.
It was now so small that the girls could
only see its blue-silver glow. Mia tucked
it into the silk pouch and put it in a
pocket in her dress.

"Will you come with me to return it?" she asked.

The girls nodded eagerly as Mia looked up into the sky. The eclipse was ending, and a single moonbeam was making a pool of light on the pavement.

"Let's go!" she said.

Holding hands, Mia, Rachel, and Kirsty stepped into the pool of moonlight. At once, the silvery glow whirled around them, lifting them gently into the air. They all closed their eyes. When they opened them again, they were floating over Fairyland!

Wedding Bells

The three friends drifted toward the
Fairyland Palace. Below, they could see
the king and queen, and all the fairies
from the Wedding Workshop. Mia and the
girls landed beside them, and Mia eagerly
pulled out the silver veil. Everyone
cheered happily.

"Great job, all of you!" cried Queen Titania.

They all hurried to the Wedding Workshop, where an archway led into a tiny, oval room with three alcoves in the wall. In the left-hand alcove, the shiny penny was sitting on a turquoise satin cushion. In the right-hand alcove, the golden bells were lying on a red silk cushion.

"This is where the silver veil belongs," said Mia. The center alcove contained a small purple velvet cushion. Mia laid the veil down there, and the whole room glowed. "Everything is in its place again," said Mia, beaming at the girls. "I have a present for you both to thank you for all your help."

She flicked her wand, and a delicate chain appeared around each girl's ankle.

"Thank you!" gasped Rachel, whose anklet had a shiny penny charm dangling off of it.

"Oh, it's beautiful!" whispered Kirsty, admiring the two gold bells on her anklet.

"I couldn't have done it without you," Mia said, hugging them.

"Now it's time

for you to get ready to be bridesmaids," said the queen. "Good luck — and thank you!"

The queen waved her wand, and Rachel and Kirsty disappeared in a sparkle of magic. All at once, they were back in their bedroom and human-size again. Sunlight was pouring in through the open window.

"It's the morning of the wedding!" said Kirsty excitedly.

Suddenly, the door burst open and Esther rushed in.

"Girls, did you manage to find the four somethings?" she asked anxiously.

Rachel and Kirsty smiled at each other. They knew exactly what to say and do. Kirsty held out her grandmother's sparkling brooch.

"Something old," she said.

"Your wedding dress is something new," Rachel added.

"Something borrowed," Kirsty said, unfastening her golden anklet.

"And something blue," declared Rachel, pulling out the bird feather they'd found in the Caribbean.

"What an amazing color!" said Esther. "It can go into my bouquet."

Rachel unhooked the shiny penny charm from her anklet and held it out.

"And a penny in her shoe!" the girls chanted together.

Kirsty and Rachel took showers and then put on their beautiful bridesmaid dresses. Mrs. Tate decorated their hair with tiny white roses. Then Kirsty and Rachel went to help Esther. She looked like a princess in her ivory dress! The girls arranged the filmy veil over her long black curls.

"Oh, girls, I'm so nervous!" Esther exclaimed.

"Don't be," said Kirsty with a happy laugh. "I just know that this is going to be an absolutely magical wedding!"

As the bride and groom stepped out of the church after the ceremony, confetti fluttered around their heads. Behind them, Kirsty and Rachel were smiling happily.

"Hasn't it been a wonderful morning?" Kirsty said. "I think my favorite part was the horse-drawn carriage that brought us to the church!"

"Mine was walking down the aisle while the beautiful music played," Rachel replied, her eyes sparkling.

Esther turned around and smiled at them.

"You've been the perfect bridesmaids, girls," she said. "Thank you!"

"Everyone say 'Cheese'!" called the photographer.

Kirsty and Rachel put their arms around each other's waists and exchanged a secret smile. They had a much better word.

"Magic!" they cried together.

SPECIAL EDITION

Don't miss Rachel and Kirsty's
other magical adventures!
Take a look at this special sneak peek of

Kylie
the Carnival Fairy!

The Carnival Begins!

"This is so exciting!" Rachel Walker said to her best friend, Kirsty Tate. "I've never been to a real carnival before."

"And Sunnydays is the *best* carnival," Kirsty replied. "It comes to Wetherbury every summer. I'm so glad you're staying with us, so that you can visit the carnival, too."

The girls were standing with a big crowd of people, including Kirsty's parents, outside the gates of the carnival grounds. The buzz of excited chatter filled the air as everyone waited for the grand opening.

"Which ride will you go on first, girls?" asked Mr. Tate.

"I don't know," Kirsty said, peering over the gates. "There are so many!" She could see a Ferris wheel, bumper cars, spinning teacups, and lots of other rides. There were also booths of food and games like the ring toss and hook-a-duck.

"Let the carnival magic begin!" announced the carnival master, sweeping off his top hat and pointing it at the

Ferris wheel. Immediately, the great wheel began to turn! The crowd gasped.

Then the carnival master waved his hat at the teacups, which began to spin in a blur of bright colors.

"It *is* magic!" gasped a little girl nearby as the rides sprang to life.

Rachel and Kirsty smiled. They knew all about magic. The two girls had become friends with the fairies!

RAINBOW magic™

There's Magic in Every Series!

The Rainbow Fairies

The Weather Fairies

The Jewel Fairies

The Pet Fairies

The Fun Day Fairies

The Petal Fairies

The Dance Fairies

Read them all!